To my niece and nephew,

Maya and Milan

The Blue Marlin Festival

藍馬林魚節

Christian Beamish 著

吳泳霈 譯

朱正明 繪

The Blue Marlin Festival was held every spring in the village where Paulo lived. People from all over the island Santiago of Cape Verde came to see the normally quiet fishing village transform into a bustling tent city illuminated by long strands of colorful lights. There was a giant Ferris wheel brought in from the other side of the island and a band played all night on a stage that was specially built for the festival.

People ate wonderful food like marlin cakes and jam pies, and they drank tasty fruit drinks as well. The men shot cork guns at the shooting gallery for tiny cups of sherry, and the women tossed rings onto bottlenecks for beaded necklaces. The children of course ran wild, free of their parents and lost in the great crowd, the music, and the lights of the festival.

This year, young Paulo and his classmates were to perform the opening ceremony for the festival. The students rehearsed for months. They made their own costumes with shiny blue suits and fish masks in honor of the Blue Marlin. The band was to play a ballad and the students would dance like Blue Marlin swimming across the stage. Although Paulo did not like dancing very much, he was proud of the Blue Marlin mask he had made and excited about performing in the festival.

Paulo woke up before sunrise on the day of the festival and watched the workmen assemble the Ferris wheel, the food and game tents, and build the music stage. The musicians gathered for a sound check at noon, but there was a problem. Sammy Selero, the great guitarist from the island of San Vicente, had cut his hand while fishing and would not be able to play.

"What are we going to do?" the bandleader asked in a loud and worried voice. He wore a beige suit with an orange silk shirt and he was sweating. "The show cannot go on without a guitar player!"

The workmen stopped putting up the tents and the musicians stood on stage. No one seemed to know what to do.

Paulo had an idea. The boy ran off in the direction of the lighthouse.

"Joaquim!" Paulo yelled when he reached the rusted front gate of the lighthouse. "Joaquim!" he yelled again.

"Up here, Paulo!" the old man called from the catwalk at the top of the lighthouse tower, where he was washing the large windows.

Paulo sprinted up the thirteen turns of the spiral staircase and stood panting and out of breath, facing Joaquim. The boy wiped his mouth with the back of his hand and said very quickly, "The bandleader said there could be no music without a guitar player!"

"What are you talking about, my friend?" the old man asked the boy.

Paulo took a deep breath and grasped the handrail of the catwalk. Slowly this time, he said, "Sammy Salero, the guitarist from San Vicente, cut himself fishing last night and he cannot play the festival."

The old man nodded his head and continued to wash the windows. "I hope Mr. Salero recovers from his injury soon," he said.

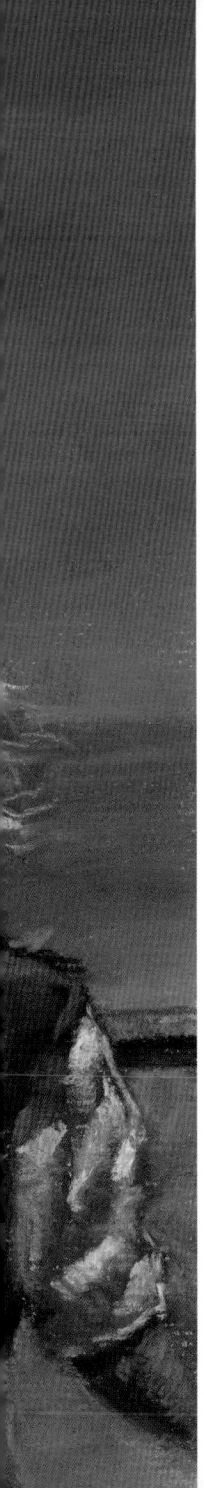

The Ferris wheel, tents, and the blue flags of the festival were visible in the distance from where Joaquim and Paulo stood on the catwalk of the lighthouse tower.

"Would you play in his place, Joaquim?" Paulo asked.

Joaquim shook his head and rubbed the windows with a sponge and hot water. He said, "I have too much to do here at the lighthouse." The old man picked up his bucket and started back down the lighthouse stairs.

Paulo followed him. "If I help you," the boy said, "we can finish in time for tonight's music!"

"Paulo!" Joaquim replied, "I do not want to play at the festival tonight!"

"But Joaquim!" Paulo pleaded, "I made my mask and prepared for the opening ceremony!"

The old man looked at his young friend and said, "I'm sorry." Joaquim turned and walked to the front door of the lighthouse. He hesitated for a moment and then turned around, but Paulo had already gone.

When evening came the lights of the festival shone as brightly as ever—red, blue, yellow and white, strung from every tent and booth. It was beautiful. The Ferris wheel turned in the darkening sky, the men shot the cork guns for their cups of sherry and the women tossed the rings for their beaded necklaces. Couples strolled and ate marlin cakes and jam pies and enjoyed fruit drinks. Throngs of people were at the festival just like every year, but this year a big sign stood in the middle of the stage that read: MUSIC CANCELLED.

Paulo stood in front of the stage with his classmates and read the sign over and over again. The musicians' chairs were still in place, the drum kit was still set up and the bass and horns all waited on their stands for the band to arrive. But the sign remained in the middle of the stage, its two words uncompromising: MUSIC CANCELLED. The kids were very disappointed that they would not get to perform.

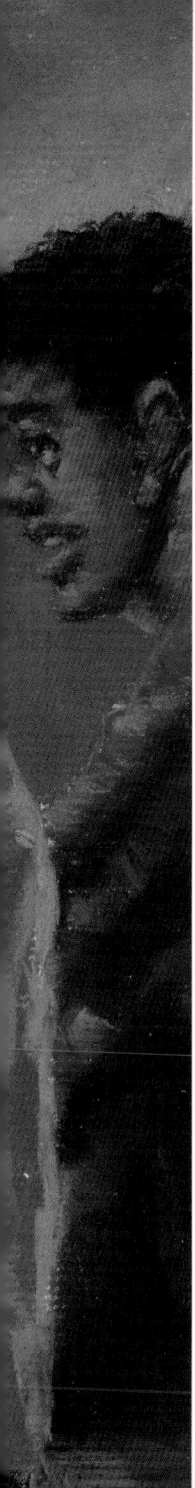

Then the bandleader with the orange silk shirt appeared and said, "Hey kids! Grab your marlin masks, the music is coming on after all!"

The kids cheered and rushed backstage to get their masks.

Joaquim walked by just as Paulo was putting his mask on. When the old man saw his friend, he said, "There you are, Paulo! After you left the lighthouse today, I realized that your performance was more important than cleaning the lighthouse."

Paulo smiled a big smile. "Thank you, Joaquim," he said, "thank you very much!"

When Paulo and his classmates danced across the stage like a school of Blue Marlin, the people in the crowd cheered wildly. There were hundreds and hundreds of people there to see the performance. The bandleader said later that it was the best Blue Marlin Festival ever.

Vocabulary

marlin [ˋmɑrlɪn] n. 馬林魚

p.2

bustling [ˋbʌslɪŋ] adj. 熙攘的
illuminate [ɪˋlumə͵net] v. 照亮
strand [strænd] n. 海灘
Ferris wheel [ˋferɪs͵hwil] n. 摩天輪

p.4

sherry [ˋʃɛrɪ] n. 雪利酒 (西班牙產的一種
烈性白葡萄酒)
bottleneck [ˋbɑtl͵nek] n. 瓶頸

p.6

opening [ˋopənɪŋ] adj. 開始的
ballad [ˋbæləd] n. 民謠，歌謠

P.8

workman [`wɝkmən] n. 工匠，工人

P.11

beige [beʒ] adj. 米黃色的

P.12

catwalk [`kæt͵wɔk] n. 狹小通道

sprint [sprɪnt] v. 衝刺；奮力而跑

spiral [`spaɪrəl] adj. 螺旋的

staircase [`stɛr͵kes] n. 樓梯

pant [pænt] v. 氣喘

P.14

handrail [`hænd͵rel] n. 欄杆；扶手

P.17

sponge [spʌndʒ] n. 海綿

P.18

plead [plid] v. 懇求

P.21

booth [buθ] n. (有篷的) 攤子

stroll [strol] v. 散步

throng [θrɔŋ] n. 大群

P.23

bass [bes] n. 低音樂器

stand [stænd] n. 看臺

uncompromising [ʌn`kɑmprə͵maɪzɪŋ]

adj. 不妥協的；堅定的

P.25

grab [græb] v. 抓取

故事中譯

P.2

　　每年春天，保羅住的村落都會舉辦藍馬林魚節。生活在維德角聖地牙哥島上各地的人，都會來瞧瞧這個平時一向寧靜的漁村，變成一個喧鬧城市的景象：到處都是帳棚並裝飾著長串色彩繽紛的燈光，還有一座從島的另一邊運來的大型摩天輪；樂隊會在特別為慶典搭建的舞台上演奏一整晚。

P.4

　　大家吃著美味的食物，像是用馬林魚做成的糕點和果醬派等，並喝著可口的水果飲料。男士們為了贏得一小杯雪利酒，聚集在靶場射軟木槍；女士們則為了贏得串珠項鍊，努力將套環擲到瓶頸上。小孩子們沒有父母管，當然更放肆了起來，隱沒在廣大的人群、音樂、和節慶的燈光中。

P.6

　　今年，小保羅和他的同學將為慶典的開幕式表演。這群學生已經排練了好幾個月。他們還自己製作舞台服裝——包括一套套閃亮的藍色衣服和魚面具，來向藍馬林魚致敬。樂隊將演奏一首民謠，而這群學生會隨著音樂跳舞，他們的舞姿就像藍馬林魚游過舞台一樣。雖然保羅並不是很喜歡跳舞，但是他對自己製作的藍馬林魚面具很自豪，更因為能夠在慶典上表演而興奮不已。

P.8

　　慶典當天，保羅在太陽升起前就醒來了。他看著工人們組裝摩天輪、準備食物、搭起供應食物和玩遊戲的棚子，並建造音樂台。到了中午，所有樂手聚在一起要試音，可是卻出了一個問題：從聖文森特島來的一流吉他手山米·塞勒羅，因為捕魚時割傷手而無法表演了。

P.11

樂隊隊長擔憂的大聲問：「該怎麼辦才好呢？」他穿著一套米黃色的西裝搭配橘色絲質襯衫，身上的汗水直流。他說：「沒有吉他手，表演就不能進行了！」

工人們停止搭帳篷的動作，所有樂手直愣愣的站在台上，似乎沒有人知道該怎麼辦。

保羅想到了一個辦法。他朝燈塔的方向跑去。

P.12

當保羅到達燈塔生鏽的前門時，他大叫：「喬昆！」然後再叫了一次：「喬昆！」

老人從燈塔頂端的窄道大聲叫：「保羅，我在上面！」他正在刷洗大玻璃窗。

保羅快速衝上這個有十三層迴轉的螺旋梯，上氣不接下氣的站在喬昆面前。他用手背抹了抹嘴巴，急急忙忙說：「樂隊隊長說如果沒有吉他手的話，可能就沒有音樂了！」

P.14

老人問他：「我的朋友，你在說什麼？」

保羅深呼吸了一口氣，抓著窄道旁的欄杆。這次，他慢慢的說：「從聖文森特島來的吉他手山米·塞勒羅，昨晚捕魚時割傷了手，所以他不能為慶典演奏了！」

老人點點頭，繼續刷洗窗子。他說：「希望塞勒羅先生的傷能早日康復。」

P.17

從喬昆和保羅站著的塔頂窄道往遠方望去，可以看到摩天輪、帳篷、和慶祝節慶的藍色旗子。

保羅問：「喬昆，你可以代替他演奏嗎？」

喬昆搖搖頭，繼續用海綿和熱水擦著窗戶。他說：「燈塔這裡有太多事得做。」老人拿起他的水桶，開始走下燈塔的樓梯。

P.18

保羅跟在他後面，對他說：「如果我幫你，我們就可以趕在今晚的音樂表演前完成了！」

喬昆回答：「保羅！我不想在今晚的慶典中演奏！」

保羅懇求著：「可是，喬昆！我自己做了面具，還為這次的開幕式作了準備！」

老人注視著他的年輕朋友，說：「很抱歉。」喬昆轉身走到燈塔的前門。他猶豫了一會兒，然後又轉過身，但是保羅已經不見了。

P.21

當夜晚來臨時，節慶的燈火像以往一樣明亮的閃耀著——紅、藍、黃、白，串連在每一個帳篷和攤位間，真是美麗極了。摩天輪在漸暗的天空中旋轉，男士們為了他們的雪利酒射著軟木槍；女士們為了得到串珠項鍊而拋擲著套環。情侶們邊散步邊品嚐馬林魚糕點和果醬派，並享受著水果飲料。就像往年一樣，大量的人群都來參加慶典；但是今年舞台中間卻立著一個大大的牌子，上面寫著：**音樂取消**。

P.23

　　保羅和他的同學們站在舞台前，一次又一次讀著那個牌子。樂手們的椅子仍放在表演位置上，成套的鼓也依然設置在那兒，低音吉他和管樂器都就定位在等待樂隊的到來。但是牌子仍然立在舞台中央，頑強的寫著那幾個大字：**音樂取消**。這些孩子們都因為不能上台表演而感到非常失望。

P.25

　　這時，穿橘色絲質襯衫的樂隊隊長出現了，他說：「嘿！小朋友們！去拿你們的馬林魚面具，音樂終於要開始了！」

　　孩子們歡呼了起來，衝到後台去拿他們的面具。

P.27

　　就在保羅要戴上他的面具時，喬昆剛好經過。當老人看到他的朋友時，他說：「保羅，你在這兒啊！你今天離開燈塔後，我才明白，你的表演比打掃燈塔來得重要多了。」

　　保羅給了他一個大大的微笑，說：「喬昆，謝謝你。真的非常感謝你！」

P.28

　　當保羅和他的同學們像一群藍色馬林魚般穿梭過舞台時，群眾們瘋狂的歡呼著。有好幾百人都來看這場表演。表演結束後，樂隊隊長說這是有史以來最棒的藍馬林魚節了！

Exercises

Part One. Reading Comprehension

_____ 1. Which of the following was NOT the activity that people did in the Blue Marlin Festival?

(A) People ate marlin cakes and jam pies.

(B) The men drank fruit drinks and sherry.

(C) The children performed the closing ceremony for the festival.

(D) The women tossed rings onto bottlenecks for necklaces.

_____ 2. What was Joaquim's first response when Paulo asked him to replace the guitarist of the band?

(A) Joaquim felt honored and said yes to Paulo's request.

(B) Joaquim felt annoyed and yelled at Paulo angrily.

(C) Joaquim asked for more time to consider Paulo's suggestion.

(D) Joaquim refused Paulo's request and then walked away from him.

_____ 3. What happened to the opening ceremony of the festival at the end of the story?

(A) The children performed the opening ceremony without music.

(B) Joaquim came to play the guitar and the festival was successful.

(C) The opening ceremony was cancelled due to the lack of a guitarist.

(D) The bandleader found someone else to play the guitar and the festival was successful.

Part Two. Topics for Discussion

Answer the following questions in your own words and try to support your answers with details in the story. There are no correct answers to the questions in this section.

1. Have you ever participated in any festivals home or abroad? What did the festival celebrate? What did people do in the festival?

2. In the story, the bandleader decided to cancel the performance due to the lack of a guitarist. What would you do if you were the bandleader?

3. In the beginning, Joaquim refused Paulo's request, but he showed up and played the festival in the end. Describe Joaquim's changes in thought and attitude.

Answers

Part One. Reading Comprehension
1.(C)   2.(D)   3.(B)

 旅遊導覽

維德角共和國 (Republic of Cape Verde)

維德角共和國位於非洲西邊的大西洋，主要是由十個大小不同的島嶼組成，因為曾是天主教國家葡萄牙的殖民地，因此節慶活動深受天主教影響；而又因為國家分屬十個島嶼，節慶習俗不盡相同，但有一些共同的國定假日如下：

- 1 月 20 日：國家英雄節 (National Heroes' Day)。
- 7 月 5 日：維德角獨立日 (Independence Day)，慶祝西元 1975 年自葡萄牙獨立。
- 8 月 15 日：聖母升天日 (Assumption Day)。
- 9 月 12 日：維德角國慶日 (National Day)，紀念幫助維德角獨立的非洲獨立黨創建人 Amilcar Cabral。
- 11 月 1 日：萬聖節 (All Saints' Day)。

除了上述國定假日之外，維德角在 5 月到 8 月間還有一些特殊的節慶活動，慶祝的方式通常是在教堂舉行宗教儀式、有音樂伴奏的集會遊行，及活動後民眾一起享用專為這些節慶準備的特殊食物等。節慶的內容如下：

- 2 月到 3 月──嘉年華會 (Carnival)
  此嘉年華會是維德角共和國最大最有名的節慶，通常在位於聖地牙哥島 (Santiago) 的首都培亞 (Praia)，及位於聖文森特島 (San Vicente) 的明德盧 (Mindelo) 舉行。嘉年華會慶祝的方式以遊行為主，參與遊行的表演人員會穿上鮮豔的服裝，戴上誇張華麗的面具及頭飾，在遊行的時候跳舞，展現肢體的美感。

> 起源
> 嘉年華會起源於歐洲，是在基督教大齋期 (Lent) 前狂歡宴飲的活動。殖民時期基督教隨著強權國家到達殖民地，一些非洲殖民地國家也沿用此習俗，並在禁止販賣黑奴後，藉此慶祝自己獲得的自由權。

● 5 月到 6 月——Tabanka

Tabanka 節在聖地牙哥島 (Santiago) 舉行。這個字的原意是「小村落」，後來引申為「四海之內皆兄弟」及「互助」的意思。Tabanka 節的精神在於幽默、歡笑及慶祝的心情，因此參與者會裝扮成上流社會的王公貴族，並用充滿幽默感的詞藻和彼此交談，處處充滿著歡笑。為了要落實 Tabanka 節歡樂的精神，即使有人不幸在節日期間過世，所有參與喪禮的人在儀式結束後，都必須要忘記悲傷和死亡，並用愉悅的心情度過這個節日。

● 8 月——Baia das Gatas 音樂節 (Baia das Gatas Music Festival)

一年一度在聖文森特島 (San Vicente) 舉行的 Baia das Gatas 音樂節受到國際的矚目。每年音樂節在 8 月初舉行的時候，總會吸引來自世界各地的音樂愛好者共襄盛舉，一起享受持續三天三夜的音樂饗宴。

● Batuku

Batuku 節源於聖地牙哥島 (Santiago)，是非洲最典型的舞蹈節慶，參與者皆為女性。Batuku 分為 txabeta 及 finaçon 兩部分：txabeta 是指女性圍坐成一圈，兩膝之間塞著一捆布，藉著兩手拍打這捆布形成的節奏，來幫跳舞的人伴奏；此時舞者早已在圓圈內等候，待節奏形成，身體便隨之擺動。finaçon 是指由一歌者唱著與此團體相關的重要事件或想法的歌，並由伴奏的女性應和，形成一唱一答的合唱。

About the Author

Born March 15th, 1969 in Laguna Beach, Christian Beamish has always been attracted to the water. His father introduced him to the ocean at a very young age and he has been surfing for more than 25 years. In 1987, after graduating high school, Christian joined the U.S. Navy and worked in a construction battalion on many overseas

projects. His Navy travels have been a very important part of his development as a writer since he was exposed to many interesting places and people. The time he spent in Cape Verde with the Navy was the basis for the Paulo and Joaquim stories: the unique culture of the islands and the way the people there are so closely connected to the sea. Christian currently lives in San Clemente, California and has plans to build an 18-foot sailboat for the next stage of his ocean development.

Author's Note: About *The Blue Marlin Festival*

Although Joaquim and Paulo are friends, I imagined the old man being most comfortable by himself at the lighthouse. When Paulo needed Joaquim's help, it was a real test of their friendship, and I wanted to have Joaquim do something more for Paulo even though the old man has already helped the boy a lot in the past. I also imagined the Blue Marlin Festival as a very exciting event for the people of Santiago. I never actually saw a festival in Cape Verde like the one I imagine in this story, but I did come across a small carnival one night in Portugal. I was driving through the countryside from Spain and the road curved through a dark oak forest with moonlight shining down through the branches. Unexpectedly, I saw a carnival around a bend and stopped and ate some food and watched the people of the small village enjoy the festivities. The Blue Marlin Festival is make-believe, but Paulo's feelings of wanting to perform the dance he'd practiced with his classmates is true of children everywhere; even though I didn't see a carnival in Cape Verde, the influence of Portugal is quite strong in the culture, and I imagined the magical carnival I'd come across that night in the forests of Portugal being transported to the warm night of Cape Verde.

關於繪者

朱正明

1959 年次，現居台北市。

年幼好塗鴉；自高中時期即選讀美工科，業畢次年 (1979) 考取國立藝術專科學校美術科西畫組，1982 年以西畫水彩類第一名畢業。

求學時期除水彩、素描技法之外，並對漫畫、卡通之藝術表現形式頗有興趣，役畢後工作項度側重於卡通、漫畫、插畫。

1999 年驟生再學之念，並於次年考取國立師範大學美術研究所西畫創作組；2003 年取得美術碩士學位，該年申請入師大附中實習教師獲准，次年 2004 年取得教育部頒發之美術科正式教師資格證書，目前仍為自由工作者身分。

愛閱雙語叢書

(具國中以上英文閱讀能力者適讀)

祕密基地系列

Paulo, Joaquim and the Lighthouse Series

Christian Beamish　著

吳泳霈　譯

朱正明　繪

中英雙語，全套五本，附英文朗讀CD

①Crazy Joaquim　瘋子喬昆
②Paulo Joins the Fleet　第一次捕魚
③The Apology　保羅的道歉
④Homecoming　歸來
⑤The Blue Marlin Festival　藍馬林魚節

一段發生在西非的島嶼上，關於友誼與成長的故事。

在西非外海小島上的海邊漁村，矗立著一座
燈塔。燈塔管理員是一個叫喬昆的獨居老
人，村民們都誤以為他是個瘋子，但八歲
的小男孩保羅卻和他成為忘年之交，並學
到許多人生哲理。本系列五個溫馨且具
啟發性的生活事件，紀錄喬昆和保羅的
友誼。清新雋永的文字，配上細緻優
美的插畫，值得您細細品味。

愛閱雙語叢書

世界故事集系列

你想知道，
如何用簡單的英文，
說出一個個耳熟能詳的故事嗎？

本系列改編自世界各國民間故事，
讓你體驗以另一種語言呈現
你所熟知的故事。

Jonathan Augustine 著

Machi Takagi 繪

Bedtime Wishes
睡前願望

The Land of the
Immortals
仙人之谷

國家圖書館出版品預行編目資料

The Blue Marlin Festival: 藍馬林魚節 / Christian
Beamish著;朱正明繪;吳泳霈譯.－－初版一刷.－
－臺北市: 三民，2005
　面；　公分.－－(愛閱雙語叢書.祕密基地系列⑤)
ISBN 957－14－4328－X　　(精裝)

1. 英國語言－讀本

524.38　　　　　　　　　　　　　　94012748

網路書店位址　http://www.sanmin.com.tw

© The Blue Marlin Festival
—— 藍馬林魚節

著作人	Christian Beamish
繪　者	朱正明
譯　者	吳泳霈
發行人	劉振強
著作財產權人	三民書局股份有限公司 臺北市復興北路386號
發行所	三民書局股份有限公司 地址／臺北市復興北路386號 電話／(02)25006600 郵撥／0009998-5
印刷所	三民書局股份有限公司
門市部	復北店／臺北市復興北路386號 重南店／臺北市重慶南路一段61號
初版一刷	2005年8月
編　號	S 805701
定　價	新臺幣貳佰元整

行政院新聞局登記證局版臺業字第○二○○號

有著作權·不准侵害

ISBN　957－14－4328－X　　(精裝)